THE GIANT PANDA

Jin Xuqi and Markus Kappeler

THE GIANT PANDA

Translated by Noel Simon

可愛的大熊猫

G. P. Putnam's Sons

New York

◆

This book is the result of close collaboration with
Xinhua Publishing House in Beijing.

We thank Xu Bang, Director and Editor-in-Chief, and his
colleagues for the scrupulous care and attention which
they gave this project, especially Jin Xuqi, who wrote
the basic text, and Xu Peide, who supervised the editing.

Kinderbuchverlag

The Chinese characters on the title page mean
"The lovable giant panda."

Copyright © 1986 by Kinderbuchverlag KBV Luzern AG
English translation copyright © 1986 by G. P. Putnam's Sons
All rights reserved. Published simultaneously in Canada by
General Publishing Co. Limited, Toronto.   Printed in Italy.
Designed by Alice Lee Groton.   First American edition 1986.
First published by Kinderbuchverlag KBV Luzern AG under
the title *Der Grosse Panda: Bedrohtes Leben im Bambuswald*.
First impression.

Library of Congress Cataloging-in-Publication Data
Jin, Xuqi.   The giant panda.   Translation of: Der grosse Panda.
Summary: Photographs and text depict the characteristics,
habitat, and behavior of giant pandas, including feeding habits
and reproduction, as well as current efforts to protect and
breed them in captivity.   1. Giant panda—Juvenile literature.
[1. Giant panda. 2. Pandas]   1. Kappeler, Markus, 1953–
II. Title. QL737.C214J5613   1986   599.74′443   86-9480
ISBN 0-399-21389-9

Photograph credits on page 48

That most appealing of creatures, the giant panda, lives in China, where one of its names is *daxiongmao*, or "large bearcat." This may seem an appropriate name, but it is misleading. The giant panda is related to the bear family, but it is not a typical bear, and it certainly isn't a cat. It belongs neither to the family of true bears, which includes brown and black bears and polar bears, nor to their relatives, raccoons, coatis, kinkajous, and other species. Most scientists place the giant panda, together with its closest relative, the lesser (or red) panda, in the separate panda family.

Pandas are tubby, round-faced animals, with small erect ears and black patches around the eyes. A panda's black-and-white coat is conspicuous, unusual and useful to the way in which a panda likes to live. Pandas are solitary animals, and their dramatic coloring helps them to avoid unintentionally disturbing one another. Although they have sensitive hearing and an acute sense of smell, their eyesight is not very good, but they can spot each other's coats at a distance against the dense vegetation of their natural habitat, and stay out of each other's way.

With their conspicuous coat and poor eyesight, one might think that pandas are easy prey to their enemies, such as leopards, brown bears, wild dogs, and hunters. However, they are extremely competent climbers. At the first sign of danger, a panda climbs into the fork of the nearest tree, where it squats on its hindquarters without making a sound. High above the ground, the black-and-white pattern of its coat is an effective camouflage. The black parts of the fur blend in with the dark trunks and branches, while the white parts become almost invisible against the bright sky. This reduces the animal's outline almost to the vanishing point, and its enemies can easily miss seeing the panda even when standing directly below it. So the dramatic markings of the giant panda not only help it to avoid unwelcome meetings with other pandas, but they also reduce the chances of its being spotted by enemies.

The giant panda's feeding habits are as unusual as its coloration. Although classified as a carnivore, it differs from most other carnivores, such as wolves and tigers, by eating meat only on rare occasions. Neither is it omnivorous like its closest relatives the true bears, which will eat almost anything.

The panda is a plant eater and it confines itself to a single group of plants, the bamboo, for its everyday diet. Now and then, the panda nibbles at other plants and it may accidentally swallow a careless bamboo rat—skin, hair, and all. But normally it feeds exclusively on the stems, twigs, leaves, and fresh young shoots of various types of bamboo.

Bamboo is related to grass, which requires the animal eating it to have a specially equipped digestive system. The cow, for ex-

Today the giant panda is found in only a few remote mountainous regions in the southwestern part of China, areas so wild that no roads have been built there. These mountain ranges rise tier upon tier in a series of gigantic steps to the Tibetan Plateau. The rugged peaks are often hidden under thick clouds, and thundering waterfalls plunge down their slopes into deep valleys.

ample, which feeds on grass, has a stomach with four different compartments, and intestines that are from 130 to 164 feet long. But the panda has the simple stomach of a carnivore with intestines that are barely 33 feet long. Because it cannot digest bamboo properly, it has to eat enormous quantities—22 to 44 pounds a day—to get enough nourishment. The panda actually spends about fourteen hours a day, summer and winter, feeding.

When the panda is not eating, it spends most of its time resting wherever it happens to be. It doesn't matter if it is day or night. When a panda is tired, it simply flops on the ground for a few hours, then wakes up and feeds for several more hours.

Pandas have an enormous capacity for water. Because so few people have seen a panda in the wild, various legends have built up around it. One of the stories explaining its enormous thirst is that the panda mistakes its own reflection in the water for another panda, and drinks as much as it can to prevent the other panda from having any. Another story says that the panda is so upset by the ceaseless babbling of the water rushing down the mountainside when the snow melts in the spring that it tries to drink the stream dry to stop the noise. The local Tibetans insist that the panda drinks water in such vast quantities that it collapses on the ground and remains in a stupor for several hours as if it were drunk. But as romantic as these stories are, there is no scientific evidence to support any of them.

In these remote mountains, covered with luxuriant forests of bamboo, the panda is at home. The bamboo on which it survives is so dense that visibility is limited to a few yards. But the thick undergrowth is criss-crossed with tunnels through which the panda can move silently and quickly and remain concealed.

Pandas live alone and each one knows its own territory well. A panda has no regular place to sleep. It simply lies on the ground wherever it happens to be when it wants to sleep. In bad weather, it may shelter in a cave or a hollow tree. Female pandas choose such places for dens when they give birth to their young.

These young pandas may live as long as thirty years and weigh as much as 260 pounds. Full grown pandas are close to 5 feet tall when standing up and some grow as tall as 5 feet 8 inches. Males and females are similar in appearance, the females being slightly smaller.

The panda's thick waterproof coat protects it from the cold in its damp, misty habitat. Its short, shaggy tail, concealed in the fur of its hindquarters, is hardly ever visible. The tail protects the panda's scent glands. It is also used to paint the animal's scent on whatever it is marking. Powerful claws help it grip the tree trunks when climbing.

The panda is seldom in a hurry. It ambles along with a rolling gait, paws turned inward and head held low. The panda usually remains on the ground, but it is an extremely agile climber and, should danger threaten, it will climb the nearest tree to safety.

Pandas feed almost exclusively on bamboo. They particularly like juicy young bamboo shoots. Many different types of bamboo are found in the mountain forests of China. This one resembles gigantic grass many yards high with a stem the consistency of wood.

The panda easily bites off and chews bamboo stalks with large molars set in jaws that are worked by powerful chewing muscles. The panda's forepaws are specially adapted for grasping bamboo stalks. In the course of evolution, the panda has developed a sixth digit on the forepaws. This so-called ''thumb,'' used with the first ''finger,'' lets the panda hold bamboo stems with great precision.

Pandas feed almost entirely on
bamboo, occasionally adding other
plants, and even fruit, fungi or bark, to
their diet. But in spite of being
habitually vegetarian, the panda enjoys
meat when he can get it. He is not a
successful hunter and has little
opportunity to help himself to the kills of
other animals. The best he can hope for is
to catch an unsuspecting bamboo rat.

The tufted deer which shares
the panda's habitat is far too
wary and alert to fall victim to
a panda. If, by chance, a
panda does feed on another
animal, the evidence will
appear in its droppings. The
droppings on the left contain
hairs, while those on the right
consist only of undigested
bamboo fibers.

China is the second largest country in the world and has the largest number of people of any nation. Within the boundaries of its habitat in that vast country, the giant panda is relatively numerous. But because these habitat areas are so limited, the panda has become an extremely rare animal on our planet.

Giant pandas live in mist-shrouded forests at an altitude of between 5000 and 11,500 feet. The vegetation is mainly bamboo, which grows in dense thickets, giving the pandas abundant food throughout the year. Mountain streams and rivulets provide more than enough water to satisfy even the panda's enormous thirst. At these heights it is extremely cold and it snows often, but the panda's thick coat protects it against cold and dampness.

Centuries ago, forests similar to those in which the panda lives were widespread in China. In those days fewer people inhabited the country. But as the population grew, forests were cleared to make way for villages and rice fields, and timber was used to build houses and to burn for cooking and heating. People hunted the black-and-white panda for its skin, which was popular as a sleeping mat. Besides being soft and warm, panda skins were believed to ward off evil spirits. So, little by little, the panda's habitat got smaller, and pandas were forced to retreat even deeper into the mountains.

Today giant pandas are found in only a few remote mountain regions in southwestern China: in the Qionglai, the Daxiangling, the Xiaoxiangling, and Liang Mountains in Sichuan Province; the Min Mountains in the Sichuan and Gansu Provinces; and in the Qinling Range in Shaanxi Province.

At most, one thousand of these "national treasures"—as pandas are officially designated—live in China today. Indeed, the giant panda is regarded as one of the world's rarest animals. The important question is whether the giant panda is likely to become extinct in the near future. Unfortunately, it is impossible to give a simple answer. All that can be said with certainty is that the survival of the last remaining pandas cannot be taken for granted, but that in China everything humanly possible is being done to safeguard them and to ensure their survival.

For a number of years the giant panda has been strictly protected by the government of China. Hunting is prohibited and carries severe penalties. Twelve panda sanctuaries, or reserves, have already been established to protect large stretches of suitable habitat and provide living space for up to 500 or 600 pandas. An important factor is the affection in which the panda is held by the Chinese people. Such widespread interest explains why, in recent years, the survival of the remaining pandas has seemed secure. The panda is a symbol of China's determination to treat the conservation of the country's wildlife and natural resources with the seriousness that it deserves.

But something has occurred that happens only once or twice a century: The bamboo began to flower in several of the sanctuaries. Whole thickets of bamboo came into bloom, looking absolutely lovely. Yet for the pandas the sight can signal disaster: Once bamboos have blossomed and formed seed, they wither and die. That is a normal part of this plant's life cycle, which recurs every few decades. Sometimes the dieback is spread over a number of years. For pandas living in an affected area, it produces a famine that lasts until the seed has germinated and young bamboo shoots have reappeared.

In the past it was easier for the pandas to survive such a catastrophe. If the bamboo in one forest died back, the animals could simply move to another where food was still plentiful, either from one mountain range to another or from the upper parts of

On the next page is a snow-covered mountainside in the Wolong Reserve with a surface area of 1240 square miles. Wolong, the largest of the twelve panda reserves in China, has a population of more than one hundred pandas. Early in 1984, bitterly cold weather caused unusual and serious problems for the pandas in this area.

the mountains down into the valleys. But today the pandas are confined to their last strongholds, and, hemmed in by human settlements and cultivated land, they have no other place to go. About two hundred are known to have died from starvation during the last few years. As long as the threat of bamboo die-back exists, there will be some uncertainty over the future of the remaining pandas.

But China has no intention of letting its favorite animals starve. A comprehensive program has already been started. In the worst-hit areas the local peasants have established feeding places where, day after day, large bales of food are put out for the pandas. Rescue teams comb the forest searching for weak or sick animals. Any they find are brought in to a panda reception camp, where they are cared for by specialists. After being restored to health, they are released into another area containing healthy stands of bamboo. Volunteers help to counter future famines by planting extensive areas with bamboo.

A team of Chinese and American scientists is working in the reserves, studying the natural history of the panda. Many details about pandas are still unknown, but the more the panda is understood, the better are the prospects for helping it. Only if everything is properly organized will the giant panda be able to overcome the difficulties facing its survival in the wild state.

Tremendous efforts are also being made in China to breed pandas in captivity, and about seventy giant pandas live in zoological gardens in China. They are the zoos' biggest attraction, and their enclosures are invariably surrounded by enthusiastic visitors. More than forty pandas have already been distributed to zoos all over the world. But the scientists know there is a great deal still to do. They are constantly searching for means of improving breeding results.

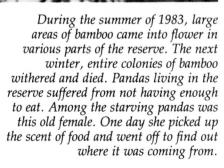

*During the summer of 1983, large
areas of bamboo came into flower in
various parts of the reserve. The next
winter, entire colonies of bamboo
withered and died. Pandas living in the
reserve suffered from not having enough
to eat. Among the starving pandas was
this old female. One day she picked up
the scent of food and went off to find out
where it was coming from.*

The female followed the scent through the deep snow until she came to a strange shelter. She could not know that she had come to the camp of a panda rescue team, which was there to help sick and starving pandas.

Nearby a man was warming himself by a fire. The normally shy panda became anxious, but hunger overcame her fear and stopped her from running away. She grabbed a stick of juicy sugar cane when it was pushed toward her and ate hungrily.

The people from the rescue team were delighted with their new arrival. She was the tamest and most trusting panda they had come across. Usually the starving pandas had to be trapped and carried on a long, tiring trek down the mountain to a holding pen at the reception camp. There the pandas could be fed until they were fit enough to be returned to the wild.

But this female stayed around without having to be caught. She found the smells from the cook's tent irresistible. Roast mutton was something new and delicious in her experience.

There is one vital disadvantage for the giant panda in eating bamboo: It has to spend a great deal of time satisfying its hunger. On the other hand, a bamboo diet also has certain advantages. Practically no other animal competes with the panda for its food, and bamboo is available in abundance at all seasons of the year, even in winter. The panda does not have to hibernate in winter because of a shortage of food, as does, for example, the brown bear. Neither is it necessary for it to collect and store winter food like the squirrel, or to migrate southward like the stork. It can remain in its habitat throughout the year and always be sure of finding enough to eat—as long as the bamboo does not come into flower. A typical panda territory is about one and one quarter to two miles in diameter. Normally the panda spends its whole life there. But it does not keep its territory entirely to itself, as many other animals do. It is not in the least put out if other pandas move in—as long as any new arrival does not come too close.

Although pandas prefer to be alone, they do meet once a year to mate. When the time comes, they "notify" one another by scent marking. As it travels about looking for food, the panda pauses in its feeding to rub its hindquarters—where there are special scent glands—against a tree trunk, stump or rock, leaving a series of scented messages for other pandas. These distinctive messages are a way of announcing that it is not far away and wishes to be left alone or that it is ready to mate.

In the holding pen, the starving pandas are fed nourishing rice gruel. They quickly acquire a taste for it and drink down entire dishfuls. Our female panda stayed for more than a month and was always tame and friendly. Every day she ate the food which had been prepared for her. When her weight had increased from 147 pounds to 198 pounds, she was taken miles away and released in an area where there was an abundance of bamboo and she could fend for herself again.

The mating instinct is strongest in the spring when the days start to lengthen, the trees come into fresh leaf, and the birds burst into song. A male panda coming across the scent marks left by a female ready to mate follows the trail. But he is careful to avoid approaching the female too closely, so as not to put her off. Unless the male can curb his impatience, the female is likely to cuff him with her sharply clawed paws, or bite his nose. She needs time in which to become accustomed to the strange male, for pandas generally have a different partner each year.

The male may have to wait a long time before the female accepts him. He sometimes shows his feelings by climbing a tree and giving a series of muffled barks and roars. At the same time he tries to impress the female with what a bold and resourceful creature he really is. His roars are intended partly for that purpose and partly to warn off other males who may be inclined to appear and perhaps disrupt the mating. It may be several days before the female is willing to accept the male. His patience is eventually rewarded and he is allowed to approach and mate with her.

The female normally crouches on the ground in front of the male with her muzzle tucked into her chest and her forepaws covering her eyes. The male squats behind her and leans upon her with his forepaws on the lower part of her back. He then mounts her and completes the mating. A short while later the two animals go their separate ways. The male has no role in caring for his offspring.

In the fall, after a gestation period of five months, the female gives birth to her young in the safety of a cave or hollow tree. Sometimes she has twins, but the second cub seldom survives.

The newborn panda is tiny. It weighs about 3½ ounces and is only 6 inches long—barely as large as a golden hamster. At first

Spring is a stimulating time of year for the panda. It is the mating season, and the males, attracted to the scents of the females, compulsively follow their tracks. But the female does not submit to the male until she has first become accustomed to him. This female has climbed a tree to escape the attentions of an impatient male. He gazes up at her, hoping that she will soon come down and allow him to mate.

the tiny cub cannot open its eyes and has no teeth. Its pale pink skin is covered with a fine down of fluffy hairs.

The female panda is a conscientious mother and devotes herself to her offspring. For the first few weeks of its life she holds the cub in her arms, never letting it go for an instant. It is completely protected from wind and weather as well as enemies. She holds it tenderly against her breast while it nurses and constantly licks it to keep it clean. The habit of carrying her young in her arms may be one of the reasons why a female panda normally raises only one cub; she would have difficulty in holding two.

The young cub grows rapidly under its mother's tender care. Its sparse covering of hair gradually thickens, and before long it is possible to make out the characteristic coat coloring. The black eye patches appear on about the sixth day, followed by the ear and shoulder markings, and last of all, the forelegs and hindlegs. After about one month the cub opens its eyes and stares around. At this stage it weighs about 2¼ pounds. At three months the cub can crawl about on its own, and its first teeth are growing in. By four months it can move about quite quickly.

In the following months the panda cub must learn from its mother all the things that it needs to know so that it can cope as an adult. For example, when danger threatens it must immediately climb the nearest tree and conceal itself in the branches. It must know where to find the juicy young bamboo shoots and learn how to bite them off, how to drink from a stream without falling in, how and where to leave its scent, and many other important matters. At the age of about 1½ years, the cub is sufficiently self-reliant to start leading an independent life. Leaving its mother, it goes in search of a suitable territory of its own. When the young panda reaches the age of five to seven years, it will look for a mate and start a family of its own.

The mating season is the only time of the year when the normally solitary pandas come together. Pandas have successfully reproduced in captivity. This is Mei-Mei, who holds her first panda baby, Ron-Shun, tenderly in her arms. The tiny rose-pink creature weighs only 3½ ounces. These two pandas live in the Chendu Zoo in China.

Ron-Shun, now seventeen days old, has a very loud voice. Normally Mei-Mei carries him in her arms, but if she puts him down, even for a moment, he screams with indignation at the top of his voice. Here Mei-Mei is trying to comfort her noisy little offspring.

Ron-Shun, at four weeks old and weighing 2¼ pounds, lies contentedly with Mei-Mei. He is no longer rose-colored and his coat has thickened and become the familiar black-and-white color of pandas. In a few weeks, he will start to crawl.

At five months old, Ron-Shun weighs 22 pounds and Mei-Mei is no longer able to carry him constantly in her arms. He must lie or sit on the ground to nurse. As he drinks, Mei-Mei lovingly licks his muzzle clean over and over again.

Ron-Shun took his first unsteady steps when he was not quite three months old. Now, two months later, he can move about like an adult, without stumbling and falling on his nose.

Ron-Shun is a playful panda who loves all kinds of tricks. One of his favorite games is to climb up on his mother's back and slide down, sometimes turning somersaults. Mei-Mei loves to cuddle her lively son.

Here is Ron-Shun when he is one year old and weighs about 65 pounds. Too old to nurse, he now likes to chew bamboo and roam around his enclosure at the zoo, where there is always something new to discover.

If Ron-Shun were living in the wild, he would soon have to leave Mei-Mei and establish his own territory. The first weeks away from a mother can be a difficult time for a young panda, but the mother has taught her offspring all he needs to know in order to live and thrive on his own.